MAR   1995

D0688261

OR

DATE DUE			
APR 14 '9	AR 05 '98		
MAY 12 '9	DEC 03 98		
MAY 22'9			
JUN 1 5 9	AN 27 99		
	SEP 16 '99		
JUL 0 3'95	FEB 07 '01		
JUL 1 3 '95			
10-9-95			
JAN 1 6 '96			
JUN 25 '9			

Jackson
County
Library
System

LITTLE PLUM

ED YOUNG

PHILOMEL BOOKS · NEW YORK

Author's Note

In China the jujube fruit is often referred to as a date or a plum. Little Plum is called *Hsiao Tso Urh* in Mandarin. It is a popular tale but, like *Lon Po Po*, it is not known to have been recorded in the classical language. There are, however, two versions from recent collections of Chinese folktales: *Zhong Guo Tong Hwa* and *Ku Tai Ming Tsiang Ku Shr Hsuan Ji*. This retelling is inspired by both of these versions.

Published by Philomel Books, a division of the Putnam & Grosset Group,
200 Madison Avenue, New York, NY 10016. All rights reserved.
This book, or parts thereof, may not be reproduced
in any form without permission in writing from the publisher.
Philomel Books, Reg. U.S. Pat. & Tm. Off.
Printed in Hong Kong by South China Printing Co. (1988), Ltd.
Published simultaneously in Canada.
Text design by Nanette Stevenson.
The text is set in Palatino.
Lettering by David Gatti.

Library of Congress Cataloging-in-Publication Data
Young, Ed. Little Plum/Ed Young.   p.   cm.
Summary: An old Chinese couple has a son who never
grows any larger than a plum seed, but his size does not
prevent him from saving his village from a cruel lord.
[1. Folklore—China.] I. Title. PZ8.1.Y84Li 1994
398.21—dc20 [E] 93-11526 CIP AC
1   3   5   7   9   10   8   6   4   2
First Impression

To Filomena
for her vision, sensibility
and support.

Once in China, in a village at the bottom of a mountain, there lived an old couple who spent their days wishing for a child of their own. One day in desperation they said they wanted a child "even if he were only as big as a plum seed."

No sooner had they made this wish than the old woman gave birth to a child, no bigger than a plum seed. The old man and the old woman were overjoyed. They called the baby Little Plum.

But as the years went by, Little Plum did not grow. He stayed the size of a plum seed. "Oh," his old father would shake his head. "What will you do, Little Plum, if you don't grow?"

"Don't worry, Father," the boy would say to his good father. "Small as I am, there is nothing that I cannot do."

This proved to be true. Little Plum could get to places no one else could. He could ride the wind to the rooftop when his father needed him there, and he helped his father gather wood and till the fields.

He would ride in an ear of the family mule. "Giddiyap," he would tell the mule. "Hoy to it," and the mule would work the fields as he never had before. Before long the stacks of wood were beyond what the family could use, and the rice and bean fields doubled their yield.

The villagers would say to their children, "Look at Little Plum. Even at his size he does more than you." The old couple was very proud of their son.

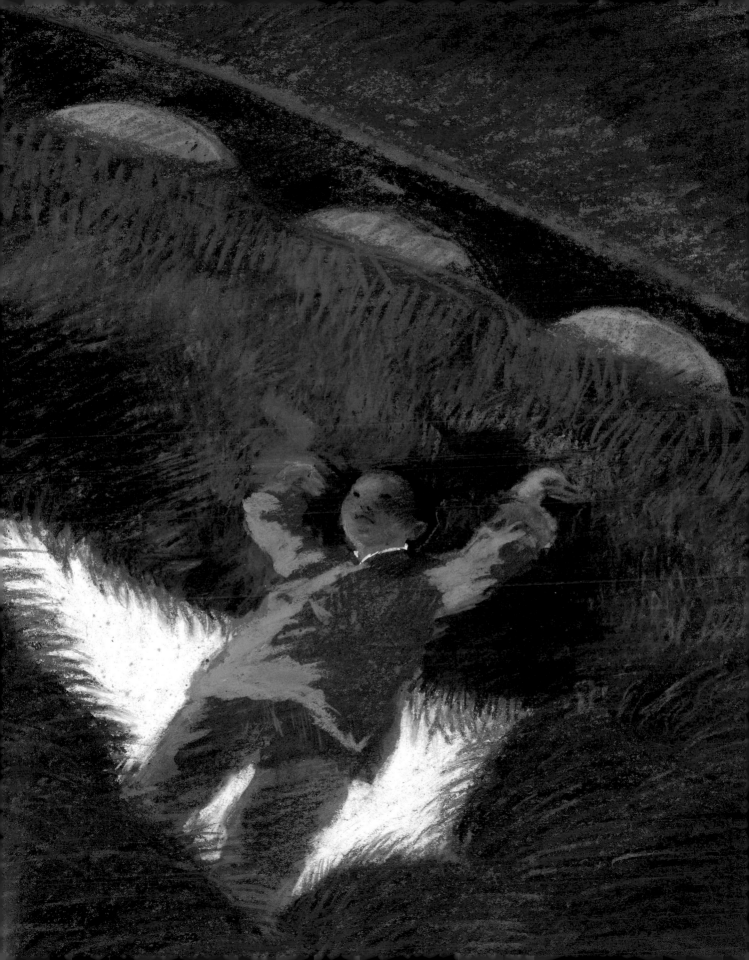

Then hard times fell upon the village at the bottom of the mountain. There was no rain and the rice and beans did not grow. Soon there was nothing to store in the village barns. When the officials from the city came to collect taxes on the grain, they found none. And so the lord of the city sent soldiers, who ran through the streets, looting and beating the villagers. When they finally left, they stole all of the livestock as well and took it to the walled city.

"Now what will we do?" the villagers cried to each other.

Little Plum climbed on the branch of a tree. "Don't worry," he said to them. "I will bring back everything."

"Little Plum," his mother scolded. "No big promises."

How could anyone so small do what he bragged!

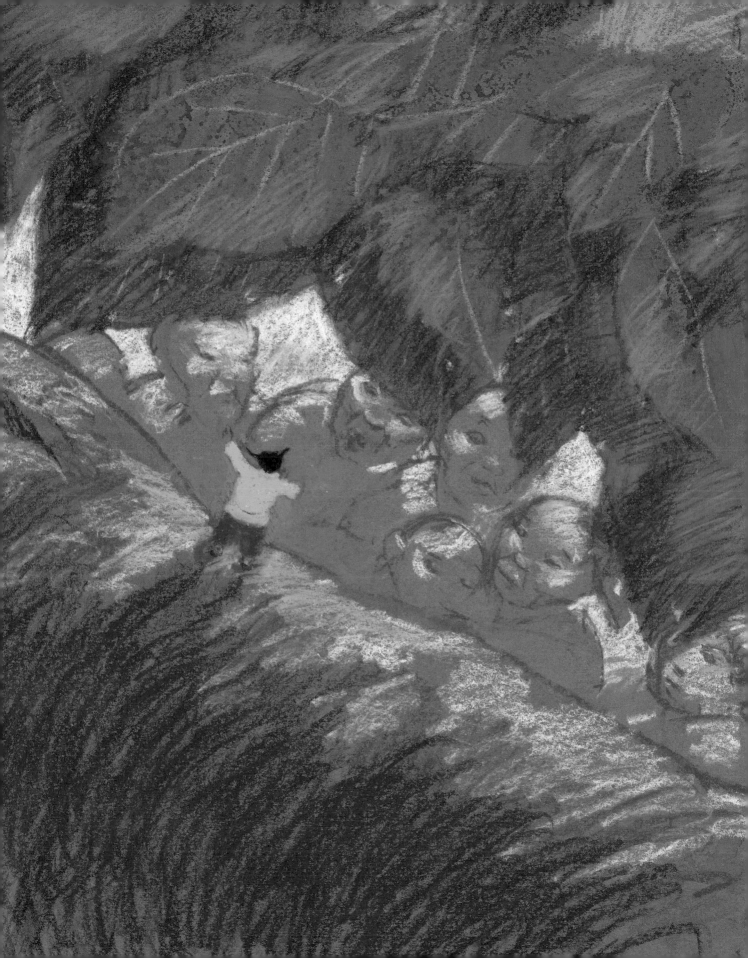

Little Plum went anyway. He had no trouble making his way across the countryside. He hunted insects for his dinner and collected dewdrops for his thirst, and arrived in only three days at the city gate.

But when he arrived, the gate was locked.

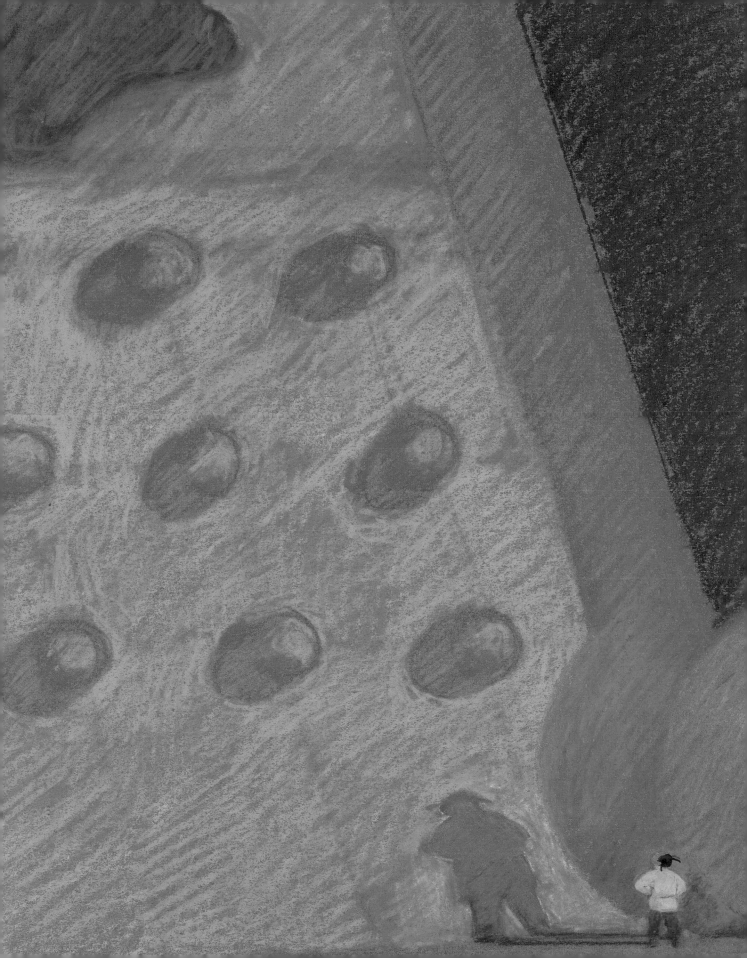

So he found a leaf, which he pulled over his head, and
let a gentle breeze blow him over the city gate.
    Then he made his way through the streets until he
found all of the stolen animals in a locked barn, with the
guards asleep outside the door.

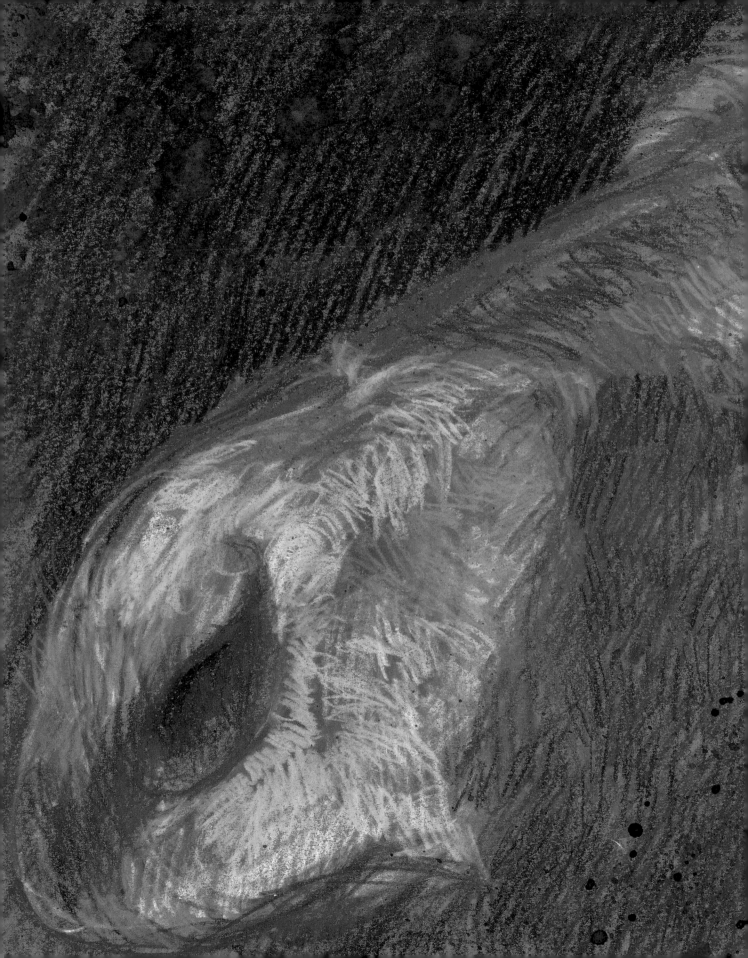

Quietly he slipped into the barn, and he saw his own mule first. With excitement, Little Plum jumped into his ear. "Oh, ho, oh, ho!" he greeted him. But he surprised the mule and it began to bray, "*Un-yah, un-yah!*"

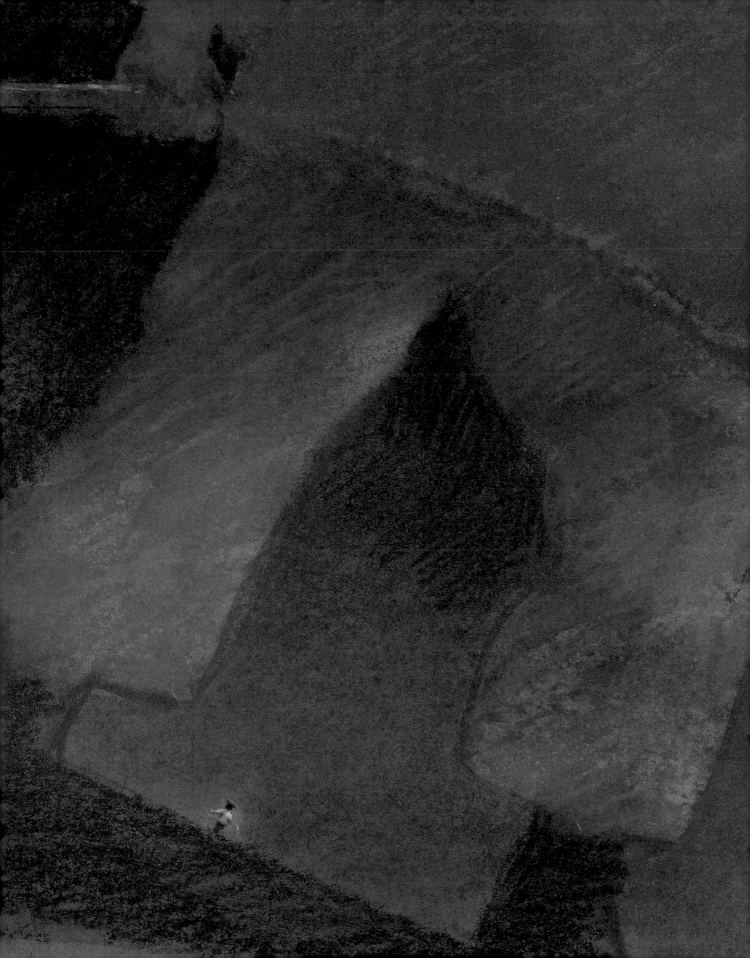

The cows began to *maw* and the sheep and goats to *bah* and *gaw*. So much commotion was there in the barn, the guards woke up and ran in.

"Thieves!" they called out. "Thieves!" They searched every post and pile of hay, but of course they could not find a thief, and so they lay down again and went to sleep.

Little Plum climbed into his mule's ear once more. But the commotion began again. *"Un-yah, un-yah,"* went the mule, now recognizing Little Plum. The cows *mawed*, the sheep and goats *bahed* and *gawed*.

Again the guards woke up and ran through the barn looking for a thief, but try as they might, they could find no one, nor could they stop the noise.

Finally, near morning, the animals quieted down and the guards fell asleep again, this time so exhausted they slept like lumps of clay.

Seeing this, Little Plum untied all of the animals, unlocked

the barn door, and, riding in his mule's ear, led all of the
animals out. "Giddiyap," he called to him. "Hoy to it!" and they
went so quickly that they all arrived home before dawn.

At daybreak the soldiers discovered the animals were gone. The lord was certain it was the work of the villagers. Angry, he called for his horse and led the soldiers back to the village again. As soon as they entered the village, they began looting and beating the people.

When Little Plum saw this, he jumped onto an earthern stand and cried out, "I am the one who returned the animals. If you must make war, you must get me first!"

"Get him," the lord said.

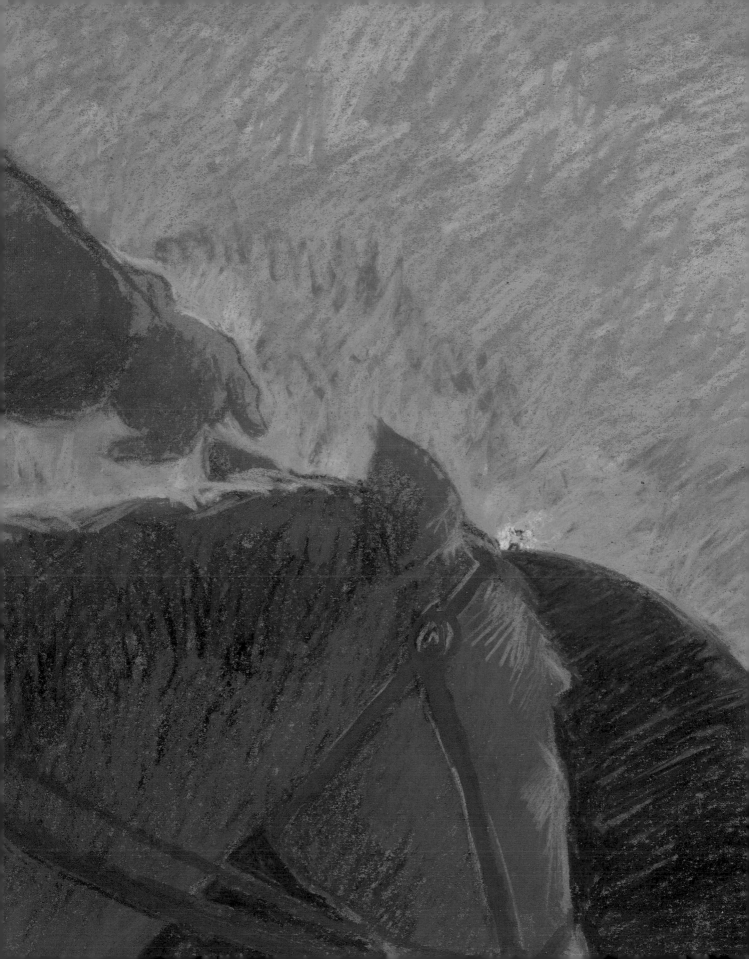

The staffs rained down on him, but Little Plum was so nimble he was never where the staffs landed. When they finally caught him and put him in chains, he slipped out of the chains, laughing.

The lord was furious. "I said, 'Get him,'" he cried.

Before the soldiers could find Little Plum, he jumped up and grabbed the lord's whiskers.

The lord pointed to his own chin. "Here he is!" he cried out. "Get him!"

And the staffs rained down on the lord's own chin.

"Enough!" he cried. "Enough," and the evil lord climbed back on his horse and led the soldiers home. He knew he had met his match in Little Plum.

All of the villagers rejoiced, but the old man and the old woman were the happiest, because they knew that Little Plum was as big as his promise; and together they lived in that place peacefully without any more trouble from the evil lord, all the days of their lives.